Busy Little Noddy

HarperCollins *Children's Books*

Noddy was always very busy driving people around Toyland.

"There goes the little nodding man," passers-by said as he drove past. "Who's he taking to the station this morning?"

"Parp-parp!" went Noddy's horn, as he hooted at three little skittles in the road. They scuttled out of the way quickly.

Noddy had a lovely little home, which he and his friend Big-Ears had built together from toy bricks. It's called House-For-One because it is so small.

In the morning when Noddy woke up he sang a song as he got ready:

I've cleaned my teeth
And I've brushed my hair,
I've polished my shoes
And I've time to spare
I've plenty of time
To nod my head.
Noddy Nod,
Noddy Nod!

One morning there was a knock at Noddy's door.

"Hello, Noddy, are you there?" It was Clockwork Clown. "Could you get out your car and take me to the Village of the Bouncing Balls? I want to get a little bouncing ball for myself," he added.

"I plan to do a good trick with the ball. I am going to walk around on it."

Noddy didn't think that was a very good idea, but he got out his car and drove Clockwork Clown to the Village of the Bouncing Balls.

When they got to the village, Clockwork Clown told Noddy to stay in the car.

"Be careful," called Noddy to the bouncing balls. "If you bounce on my car you will flatten it and me!"

But the balls didn't listen, they kept bouncing.

Noddy thought he would drive off and hide. There were so many balls bouncing around that Noddy couldn't see where he was going.

"Whoooooooooo!" a funny noise came from one of the balls. It had a hole in it and all the air was coming out.

This made the other bouncing balls very unhappy. Clockwork Clown hurried up to the car and jumped in.

"Quick, Noddy," he cried. "Let's get out of here!"

Noddy drove home quickly. He didn't stop until he reached Toy Town Square.

"Thank you for taking me to the Village of the Bouncing Balls," said Clockwork Clown. "Here's double your fare for all your trouble."

When Noddy got home he found Gobbo, one of the Goblins, waiting for him.

Gobbo wanted Noddy to drive into the Dark Woods at midnight and pick him up. Noddy wasn't very sure. He knew what kinds of tricks the Goblins could get up to. But Gobbo offered him a bag of coins.

Noddy agreed to pick Gobbo up that night in the Dark Woods.

Just before midnight, Noddy got into his little car and set off through the streets of Toy Town. It was dark and Noddy was a little bit nervous.

"Oh," thought Noddy to himself. "I don't think this is a very good idea."

When Noddy got to the Dark Woods he thought he could hear somebody singing a funny little song:

It isn't very good
In the Dark, Dark Wood
In the middle of the night
When there isn't any light;
It isn't very good
In the Dark, Dark Wood.

Noddy began to get really scared.

"Hello, Gobbo, are you there?" called Noddy. He called again and again as he went deeper and deeper into the Dark Woods, but got no answer. He was just about to turn around when Gobbo and Sly jumped out in front of him!

"Here I am, Noddy," said Gobbo. "Now you are going to give us your car and go away!"

Poor Noddy didn't know what to do. So he got out of his car and the Goblins leapt in and drove off.

Noddy was all alone in the Dark Woods. He remembered the words of the Goblins' song and felt very frightened. He began to wander through the Dark Woods calling out for help. But no one answered.

Just as he was about to give up, he saw a light shining through the trees.

As Noddy got closer and closer to the light he began to recognise the house.

"It's Big-Ears' Toadstool House!" cried Noddy. "Big-Ears, are you there? Let me in, please."

Noddy told Big-Ears the sad story of how the Goblins had laid a trap for him and stolen his car.

"Let's hurry back to Toy Town and tell Mr Plod, the policeman, what has happened," said Big-Ears, bundling Noddy out of the door.

The two friends woke up a sleepy Mr Plod who listened to their tale with a very puzzled look on his face.

"Don't you worry, Noddy," said Mr Plod. "First thing tomorrow morning we shall look for your car. Now go home and get some sleep."

The next morning Big-Ears told Noddy he had a very good idea about how to find his car.

Big-Ears proudly showed Noddy a big notice.

Will anyone who hears
Noddy's horn go "Parp-Parp!"
please tell Big-Ears.

"Oooh!" cried Noddy. "You think the Goblins will toot the horn in my car and it will give away their hiding place? That's a very good idea, Big-Ears!"

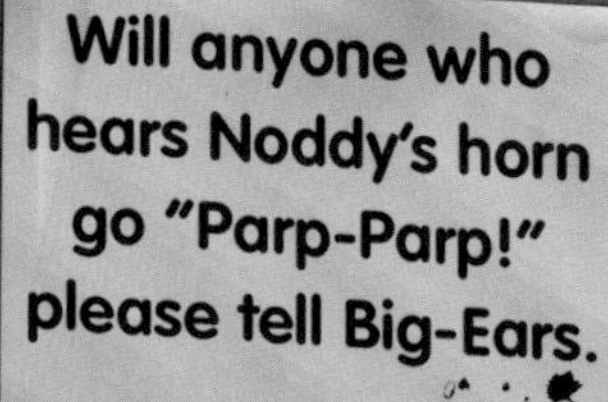

It *was* a very good idea. Master Tubby Bear knocked at Noddy's door.

"Hello, Big-Ears," said Tubby Bear. "I think I know where the Goblins are hiding Noddy's car. I was out walking in the Woods and I heard a 'parp-parp!' sound, just like Noddy's horn, coming from the old hollow tree."

"Well done, Tubby Bear," said Big-Ears happily. "Don't worry, Noddy, we will have your car back in no time."

Big-Ears went straight to find Mr Plod. Together they headed into the Dark Woods to the old hollow tree.

When they got to the tree Big-Ears and Mr Plod began to talk very loudly.

"Did you see Mr Jumbo's car by the side of the road as we came past, Mr Plod?" asked Big-Ears.

"Yes, Big-Ears," replied Mr Plod. "If Mr Jumbo isn't careful somebody will steal it!"

Big-Ears and Mr Plod knew that the Goblins wouldn't be able to resist going to take a look at Mr Jumbo's car. Sure enough, the Goblins began to crawl out of the tree. Unluckily for them, Mr Plod was there to catch them and he whisked them straight off to jail.